SILVER AND PLUM
AND OTHER STORIES

Translated from the Original Chinese

SILVER AND PLUM AND OTHER STORIES

FAIRY TALES FROM TANG TANG

TANG TANG

Illustrated by
LÜ QIUMEI

Translated by
LI XIAOCHUN

Edited and Adapted by
REBECCA MOESTA

Creative & Translation Consultant
DENNIS JI DING

EBook ISBN: 978-1-68057-307-7
Trade Paperback ISBN: 978-1-68057-306-0
Hardcover ISBN: 978-1-68057-308-4
Casebind ISBN: 978-1-68057-309-1
WordFire Press Edition 2022
Cover design by Janet McDonald
Cover artwork images by Lü Qiumei
Library of Congress Control Number: 2022935710
Published by WordFire Press, LLC
PO Box 1840 Monument CO 80132
Kevin J. Anderson & Rebecca Moesta, Publishers

CONTENTS

SILVER AND PLUM

Silver had a simple heart, as simple as his form.

He was a wooden kitten, small enough to fit in a child's hand. His body was made from only two pieces of wood fitted together, a square flat piece for the head, and a longer flat piece for the body. Not even a tail. But his triangular ears and large round eyes made it obvious that he was a cat. His golden eyes stayed open morning and night.

For many years Silver's simple heart held only two things: a promise and a master.

His master's name was Yingu. When Yingu was young, he would tuck Silver into his coat pocket and touch him every now and then, which made Silver happy. A master could own countless things: clothes, bowls, cups, a bed, pillows, toys ... Yingu was the master of many things, yet Silver had only one master.

One day Silver rolled under the bed and stayed there for many days and nights. He never saw his master search for him, but what did it matter? He could smell the young man, and he was a wooden kitten with a master.

Then came the worst part. Yingu moved away, but Silver did not. The new owner of the house came, and after a thorough cleaning, Silver and a pile of dust and debris were whisked out the door to a new destination: a trash bin by the side of the road. Silver missed the bin and fell on the ground.

Silver was confused for a long while before he realized, *Oh my god, I have no master!* He was at a loss.

Without a master, what am I? he asked himself.

I am nothing without a master, he concluded after thinking for a few days. This sort of reasoning did not make him unique, since these are exactly the same thoughts that all discarded things in the world have.

I wish I could just disappear, he thought, leaning against the trash bin. Of course, he couldn't disappear right away, since wood tends to last a long time. If he could shut his eyes maybe he would feel better, but poor Silver couldn't even do that. All he could do was keep his rounded eyes wide open, passing endless days in lonely sadness, until he turned numb and rotted and faded away. How awful!

Suddenly Silver remembered the promise.

It was the only thing left in his simple heart.

How good it was to have a promise, not just emptiness!

How long ago it had been ...

* * *

In Silver's heart, the place called Yunhe was the most beautiful in the world. He had been born there along with Plum in a wooden toy factory.

He and Plum had both belonged to a girl named Meizhu.

Meizhu and Yingu lived in the great mountains of Yunhe, their entire village bordered by mountains on all sides. Terraced fields flowed from mountain foot to mountaintop in rippling layers like ocean waves.

Yingu and Meizhu were best friends.

One day, Yingu said that he had found a lovely spot, so he took Meizhu's hand and off they ran. The soft ridges curved and turned as they worked their way up the mountain side, layer by layer. It was early summer, and the fields glistened with bright waters and delicate green shoots. A Chinese yew sat almost at the top. No one knew quite how old the tree was, probably hundreds of years, and it was so wide that three or four people could have reached their arms around it without their fingertips touching. One thick branch stood out from the others, and Yingu and Meizhu climbed up and sat on it, shoulder to shoulder.

A thin layer of mist rose out of the valley, like white gossamer blown by the wind. The thousand-year-old rice paddies flowed from the mountaintops to the mountain feet, the ridges dancing softly and embracing each other. The shining water of their arms formed mirrors of all shapes and sizes that reflected the sky and the clouds along with the new rice shoots.

"It's lovely," said Meizhu.

"We can come here often from now on," said Yingu.

"But I'm going away to the city to stay with my aunt while I go to school," she said.

Yingu was stunned and sat silent for a very long time.

Meizhu fished two wooden kittens out of her pocket and put one in Yingu's hand. Her aunt had bought them on Yunhe Street and sent them to her. The two kittens looked exactly alike, one in a darker shade of wood and one in a lighter color, and both had golden eyes so large that they took up most of the face. Although they were simple, their indescribable sweetness delighted people from the first glance.

"Let's give them names."

"Okay."

"Mine is called Plum."

"Then I'll call mine Silver."

They let Plum and Silver sit next to each other on the branch beside them.

"At this time next year, we will come here to see the view," said Meizhu.

"At this time next year, we will come here to see the view," said Yingu.

They didn't hear the two wooden kittens whispering to each other on the tree branch.

"How lovely—I have a name! I am Plum."

"How lovely—I have a name, too! I am Silver."

They each had a name and a master and a heart that beat with joy.

They touched their heads gently together and said, like their masters,

"At this time next year, we will come here to see the view."

"At this time next year, we will come here to see the view."

They heard their masters say, "Pinky promise, and don't forget for a hundred years."

So Plum and Silver also said, "Pinky promise, and don't forget for a hundred years." They nestled together with two things in their hearts: a promise and a master. They were satisfied.

Then Meizhu took Plum with her to Yunhe City. Not long after that, Yingu moved with his family to a place outside Yunhe, and they did not see each other again.

Every summer Silver anxiously cried out, "Master, master, go back to the village." Summer after summer he shouted, but his master never listened. Yingu seemed to have forgotten. It is not unusual for children to forget promises. They constantly grow and change and have many things to keep in their hearts.

How good it was that Silver still had a promise in his heart, not just emptiness!

The promise lifted Silver's spirits and made him feel different from all the other discarded things.

He straightened his crooked body and stared at the road in front of him.

He didn't have a master anymore. He didn't belong to anyone. If he didn't belong to anyone, then he belonged to himself. He was his own.

"Am I my own?" He felt a little shy and not quite used to the idea.

"Then—I can go keep that promise?" Silver moved his body. Back when he belonged to Yingu, he wasn't supposed to move at all—which is the basic nature of all inanimate belongings. It felt good to move. Was this "freedom"? When he was with Yingu, Silver hadn't thought about it much, and when Yingu left, Silver had not thought about much at all, because of his sadness.

His golden eyes held a vision of Plum, and he said happily, "I am setting off."

Alas, his simple heart forgot that the promise had been made and broken long ago, and he did not know how far it was to Yunhe. He *did* know that if he asked for directions first and then traveled in the right direction, he would get closer and closer.

He did not mope about his body's flaws. For example, he did not have four flexible legs like a real cat—just a few grooves that were supposed to look like legs, but he couldn't spread them apart to walk. He had to hop, half an inch at a time.

Silver didn't care that he could only hop in half-inch steps. He would go.

But he had to ask for directions first. Who could he ask? He glanced around and saw an ant.

"Hello, do you know which direction Yunhe is?"

"I am not interested in any direction except the direction of my food," replied the ant.

Another ant passed by, and Silver asked, "Hello, do you know how to get to Yunhe?"

"I'm sorry, I don't."

Silver thought, *One ant didn't know. Two ants didn't know. But that doesn't mean none of them know.*

He waited by the side of the road and when a long line of ants came along, he asked them one by one.

One big-headed ant pointed with its antennae and said, "Go that way."

Silver thanked the ant and happily hopped forward, half an inch at a time. He hopped for countless days and nights until a large river blocked his path. That ant with the big head must have thought Silver was looking for the Yunhe *River* and had honestly been doing its best to help. Silver stared disconsolately at the surging river and worried about how he would ever cross it. His simple mind didn't come up with an answer right away, but he kept trying.

In fact, there was a bridge not far away, but he was too small to see it.

A bird flew down and sat beside him.

"Do you know how to cross the river?" Silver asked in a hurry.

"Why would you want to cross the river?" asked the bird.

"I'm going to a place called Yunhe."

"Yunhe sounds far away. You won't get there if you go this way."

"But an ant told me I *would* get there if I went this direction."

"An ant never travels a mile from its nest. How could it know?"

Silver decided that the bird was making a great deal of sense, so he said, "You fly far—you must know."

"I don't."

Silver thought, *Just because one bird does not know, that doesn't mean all birds do not know.* So he looked up and called to every bird flying overhead, "Hello, do you know where Yunhe is?"

His voice was too small for most birds to hear, but a low-flying bird did, and landed in front of him. "I've heard of that place, though I've never been there. Why do you want to go?"

Silver told his story quite earnestly.

When he finished the bird sighed. "You won't get there."

"I'll ask the other birds," Silver said. "Someone must know."

The bird looked at his wide, innocent eyes and took pity. "Go ask the winds—they blow almost every-where."

Silver's luck was good—he got directions from the first wind he asked.

"Yunhe is to the south," the wind told him.

"I know where it is now! How happy I am!"

"Why would you want to go to Yunhe?"

Silver solemnly explained his promise to Plum.

The wind laughed, creating a tornado that swept Silver up into the air. Luckily, he was so small that when he fell to the ground, he bounced a few times and then stood up.

"How could you ever get there, little fellow?"

"It's there and it doesn't move. If I walk and it stays still, I'll get there." Silver's simple heart had already drawn a line connecting himself to Yunhe, and he imagined himself hopping straight along that line, making it shorter inch by inch.

The wind looked into his simple eyes and said, gently, "You can't get there in a straight line, silly thing. Ah, the world is full of detours, and there will always be something in your way. You're so small that it would be hard work just to get around a cow patty."

"The road will always get shorter and shorter," Silver said.

The wind froze. He had blown all over the world, and yet never met anyone so foolish and simple, or anyone who spoke wiser words.

The wind was moved. "Let me give you a ride."

So Silver flew, somersaulting with delight in the wind. He had never thought he would fly one day.

This wind passed him on to another wind. "Hey! Take this little fellow to Yunhe—a place as beautiful as a fairytale."

One by one the winds passed Silver along and delivered him where he wanted to go.

And so it was that Silver got back to Yunhe, back to the foot of that Chinese yew.

It was early summer, and the fields from the mountaintops down into the valleys sparkled with water and green grass. The grass made the water green, and the green water reflected the sky and the trees and the clouds, and the whole world was clear and bright.

Silver stood under the tree and shouted, "Plum, I'm here!"

"Silver, are you here?" Plum looked down from her perch in the tree.

Meizhu had never brought her back in all the years since they left. It was very common for a child to forget a promise. Meizhu had left Plum on a windowsill, until one day a gust of wind blew her downstairs. She lay alone in a damp corner by the wall. Moss grew all over her, yet Meizhu never came searching.

One night a mouse carried her off but dropped her again halfway to where it was going.

Plum could hardly believe that she was a kitten without a master. Like Silver, she was simple-hearted, and without her master, her only thought was of the promise.

So she set off.

She hopped along, half an inch at a time, and a curious raven with a large beak followed her for a year.

Finally, he couldn't help asking, "Where are you going?"

Plum solemnly told her story.

The raven thought the promise so beautiful that he wept. He had never had a beautiful promise of his own, so he decided to help her.

The raven scooped her up with his large beak and carried her into the mountains of Yunhe. There were many mountains and many trees, and they spent a whole year searching for the right one. When at last they found the Chinese yew that was so old it couldn't get much older, the raven plopped her on a branch, wished her good luck, and flapped away.

Plum was alone in the old yew for many summers. She waited happily every day, without anxiety or disappointment. There was only one thought in her head: Silver would come.

Plum was up in the tree. Silver was at the foot of the tree.

Silver was only a wooden kitten—he couldn't climb up the tree. He jumped and jumped at the tree trunk but bounced off of it. He jumped again and knocked against the same trunk.

His antics made a squirrel giggle, and when it stopped laughing, it carried him up the tree on its back.

Large golden eyes looked into large golden eyes. The promise was long overdue, but what did it matter? They hopped toward each other, half an inch at a time, until their heads gently came together.

And when their heads lightly touched, in a world far, far away, the adult Yingu and Meizhu, who had grown up apart, suddenly felt their eyes fill with tears. What was happening? They wiped their eyes and put their hands over their hearts, trembling with wonder—as if swept up in the tender magic of the story that was happening.

THE GHOST IN THE JASMINE
COAT

Flyyyyyy—"

Lolo sped across Flower Street, arms wide open, chin slightly raised, and with the sounds of rumbling cars and screeching tires all around her. Ten seconds later, she stood on the sidewalk, bitterly disappointed. A river of bicycles and motorcycles and cars flowed past her.

Every day since her father's disappearance, Lolo "flew" back and forth across this river of traffic.

"I'm flying!" Lolo spread her arms once more. The passing cars looked like fierce beasts. All of a sudden, her arms were caught in a vise-like grip, her feet were yanked off the ground, and she shot like a bullet across the city sky.

Her arms ached, and the wind was so sharp and

hard that even with her eyes open, she couldn't see anything.

Finally, her feet touched solid ground, and the iron grip on her arms loosened.

She found herself on a small island in the middle of a rapid river. Everyone in Flower City knew the stories about a ghost in a flower-patterned trench coat who lived on this island. Legend had it that his house had a domed roof, and the inner walls were full of shelves that displayed countless identical bowls. The ghost in the flowered trench coat never approached anyone, let alone hurt them, so the fear with which people spoke of him was based partly on truth and partly on superstition. Some people acted afraid of him and some did not.

Lolo and her father used to look out at this island in the Flower River from afar, and she had buried herself in his arms.

"Will the ghost eat me? I'm scared, Papa."

"Don't be—I am with you."

It felt like a long time since she last heard that voice, but it still rang clearly in her ears.

In any case, the legendary ghost in the flowered coat had brought Lolo to that same island. His trim green trench coat was dotted with white jasmine flowers. Lolo could not tell what he looked like, since a white mask hid his face. She didn't feel frightened, though, and she reached out to touch the jasmine flowers on his coat.

The ghost gave her a hard rap on the head. "How dare you!" he said in a fierce voice.

Lolo was indignant. "Who do you think you are? *You* brought me here! Why?"

"I wanted to."

"But why did you capture *me*?"

"I can do as I want to."

"*I* want to go back!" Lolo yelled.

"You can't." The white mask hid the ghost's expression, yet a sly glint shone in his eyes.

Lolo began to cry.

The ghost in the jasmine coat simply observed her.

As Lolo wept, she suddenly remembered how long it had been since she last cried like this. She had only cried in such an unguarded and indulgent way in front of Papa. The thought of her father drove her voice an octave higher.

The ghost watched patiently. Once Lolo finished crying, he said, "I'll give you one task. Complete it, and I'll let you go. Fail, and you'll have to live with me on this island forever."

The ghost in the floral coat led Lolo into his dome-roofed house. Inside were many rows of wooden shelves, just as the legends said, and the bowls on the shelves looked exactly the same. Each bowl was green and held a jasmine plant adorned with snow-white blossoms.

There had been a jasmine bush in Lolo's front yard,

but it was dead now, all dry and yellowy with withered branches. It must have died after Papa disappeared.

"Stop gawking, you idiot!" the ghost snapped.

"I'm dazed. What does it matter?"

"Because you must concentrate on what you have to do next." The ghost seemed displeased about something.

"I'm not interested," Lolo said, her eyes still fixed on a bowl of jasmine in bloom.

"Listen to me, Lolo. All you have to do is raise these bowls of jasmine plants, until they are able to talk. The day they begin to speak is the day you can leave this island. Otherwise, you will have to stay here until you're an old woman."

"Raise bowls?"

"Of jasmine, yes!"

"Until they can talk?"

"Yes!"

"How can bowls talk?"

"How can you have so much to say, girl?" the ghost scolded as he handed her a slip of paper. There was something on it:

How to Raise Bowls of Jasmine

1. *In the morning, take them outside and sun them. They like to feel the warmth.*

2. *At dusk, place them under the jasmine bushes. They like to smell the fragrance.*
3. *At night, set them on the lawn. They like to hear the crickets sing.*
4. *Repeat these steps every single day, and the bowls will start to talk.*

The idea was so extraordinary that Lolo, who had not cared about anything for a long time, began to perk up and take interest. Until now she had lost interest in almost everything. Only one thing had been able to draw her attention and keep it—"flying" across the street once every day through the fierce river of cars.

That was where Papa had disappeared.

Lolo had said goodbye to her father one morning before school. After that, all she saw was a box. Papa had had a car accident on Flower Street, and Grandma did not let her see him one last time, believing that the sight would overwhelm Lolo. A little black box had replaced her father. But how could her father be a box?

Lolo was ten years old and thought constantly of her father. Grandma took her to the street where Papa had his accident and told her that his spirit was floating above it. Lolo still thought of him endlessly. She raced through the traffic on Flower Street every day, wishing that her soul would join his above the street.

But now the ghost in the flowered trench coat had brought her here.

"You will live here from now on. I must be going. I need to find my treasure," the ghost said.

"Treasure?"

"Don't even ask. You must remember to do everything the slip of paper tells you to, every single day. Otherwise they get angry, and when they get angry, they shatter. If they shatter, then I will shatter too, and there will never be a ghost in a jasmine coat in the world again." As soon as the words left his mouth, he shot like a floral bullet right through the roof into the sky and was gone.

Lolo was left alone on the island, but she felt no fear. The jasmine flowers growing in the bowls were strangely comforting. For some reason, they made her feel as if Papa was very, very close, and the peaceful feeling lulled her to sleep.

She awoke the next morning, with the sun bright and gentle. Following the instructions on the paper, Lolo stacked the bowls and carried them outside. She set them down one by one and counted them—precisely one hundred bowls. Sunlight flowed over the bowls and over her. The scene suddenly felt familiar.

Ah yes, her father had loved to take her out into the sun. Whether it was winter or summer, whenever Lolo was downhearted, Papa would say, "Let's go lie in the sun." Her unhappiness would vanish as soon as the sunlight touched it. When Lolo was six, Mama had left to go abroad and said she would never come back. After that, Papa used to spread himself out on the lawn in the yard, with his arms flung wide. The sun poured thickly over him, and after a while his smile returned. He became both mother and father, and Lolo never felt abandoned because of Mama leaving.

She lay down beside the bowls, spread herself out like her father used to, and felt the sun pour thickly over her.

At twilight, she carried all of the bowls and set them beneath the low jasmine bushes behind the house, as the paper had instructed. The blossoms smelled so good in the early evening, reminding Lolo of how the jasmine in her yard had smelled. Her father used to pick jasmine flowers one by one, string them into a necklace, and slip it over her head.

Breathing in the strong scent of the flowers, Lolo grinned.

When night came, Lolo laid the bowls out on the lawn as the paper directed and sat quietly beside them. Soon she heard the soft serenade of the crickets. It was fine and sweet and crisp and bright and velvety—each cricket's song different. Papa had taught her to tell them apart when he used to take her out to catch crickets on the lawn.

Every morning, the jasmine bowls basked in the sun, and so did Lolo. The bowls breathed in the scent of jasmine at dusk, and so did Lolo. At night they listened to the crickets sing, and so did Lolo. She felt somehow that her father was close to her, and she felt more optimistic each day.

Her heart grew happier day by day, and yet the bowls did not change.

How could a bowl of plants ever talk? In her heart, Lolo admitted she did not believe such a thing was possible. Even so, she wanted to stay with the bowls day after day, lying beneath the sun, smelling jasmine blossoms, listening to cricket song. It was as though Papa was very close—as if she couldn't see him, but he saw her.

One evening at nightfall, when Lolo was sniffing flowers one by one, the ghost in the flower-patterned coat shot down from the sky like a bullet. His feet had hardly touched the ground before he exclaimed, "Go away! I've changed my mind."

Lolo was shocked. "Why?"

"No reason. Don't you want to leave?"

"No, I've changed my mind as well. I like it here."

"You can't. It's not convenient for a ghost to live with a little girl."

"But these bowls you told me to raise, they don't talk yet," she reminded him.

"I'll raise them myself. Let's go." The ghost reached out to grip her arms.

Lolo began to wail. She cried in that unguarded and indulgent way that she only did in front of her father. The ghost listened to her patiently.

By the time she was done crying, stars had appeared and were strolling languidly in the sky.

"We can sit on the grass tonight, and I will take you home tomorrow," the ghost offered.

"Must I leave?"

"Yes."

"But I don't want to. I can smell my father here."

"I know all about your father," the ghost said, "and I know why you keep running around on Flower Street. You are a very foolish girl."

Lolo raised her head. "You knew all along?"

"Ever since the first time I saw you running in the street, I've followed you. That's why you never had any accidents."

"No wonder those cars never hit me ..."

"You break your father's heart when you do that."

"He knows?"

"Of course he does. He's always close to you, even though you can't see him."

Dewdrops descended and came to rest on the blades of grass and on the rims of the bowls of jasmine. The song of the crickets became rich and mellow.

"Uncle Ghost—can I call you that?"

"Of course. A ghost doesn't care what people call him."

"Can these bowls really talk?"

"They can. To be honest, I've never heard them before. But I believe they can talk."

"What will they say?"

"Oh, I don't know."

"What's the treasure you went searching for, Uncle Ghost?"

"My daughter."

"Your *daughter*?"

"Yes. She is my treasure, and I miss her. She ran away from home, playing hide-and-seek with me. You see, she broke a bowl once, and I hit her. She left while I was sleeping. But I'm sure she'll be back. I'm her Papa— she'll miss me, don't you think?"

"She will miss you. I've been angry at my father too. Once I even stayed out all night on purpose ..." Before she knew it, she fell asleep nestled against her Uncle Ghost.

The ghost in the jasmine coat sat motionless, afraid that any little movement might wake her. They stayed like that until the sun rose and half of his body was numb.

Lolo opened her eyes. "You're sending me away soon, aren't you?"

"Yes, your grandmother is sick with worry. And your father—the one you can't see?—wants to see *you* at home, on the lawn in your yard, and on your way to school."

"I love him. I miss him."

"Then don't hurt him."

"Hurt him?"

"You hurt him when you are unhappy, and when you run recklessly across Flower Street. It cuts your father like a sword in his heart."

"Then take me home, Uncle Ghost."

The ghost in the flowered green trench coat reached out and took hold of Lolo's arms.

All of a sudden, the bowls began to talk. "I am near you. I am near you. I am near you." They really spoke! "I am near you. I am near you."

The ghost and Lolo froze. Then, almost in the same instant, they squatted down beside the bowls to listen. "I am near you. I am near you."

The ghost said his daughter was talking. "She is near me," he said.

Lolo said, "It's Papa. He says he is close to me. He's here for me."

They listened in silence for a long time, until the bowls got tired and stopped talking.

The ghost in the jasmine coat took Lolo back to her small yard.

"Can you take off your mask, Uncle Ghost? I want to see your face."

"Of course not."

"I thought you would look like my father if you took off the mask."

"Goodbye, you silly girl! Just put a jasmine flower in your buttonhole when you miss me, and I'll come take you to my island to play."

As he left, the ghost in the flowered coat blew on the wilted jasmine bush in the yard.

The next morning when Lolo stepped outside, the rich scent of jasmine flowers surrounded her. She would never hurt her father again, even though she could not see him.

FEATHER

I. The Feather

Great mountains surrounded a valley, and in this valley was a village. Through the village, down from the east end of a mountaintop, flowed a lively stream, clear and bright and noisy.

One day, the current carried down a slender, colorful feather. A girl named Long found the feather.

"Ah, this must be a phoenix feather! I've never seen one more beautiful—only a phoenix could have such lovely feathers. How lucky I am to find one!" Long cried happily and ran home with the feather to show her grandmother.

Grandma looked at it and said, "It must be a

pheasant feather—a very large pheasant. It is really very pretty."

"It's not a pheasant feather, Grandma! You told me that a phoenix lives in these mountains."

"Silly girl, that is only an ancient legend, and ah ..."

Long had heard her grandmother tell the story countless times. A long, long time ago, according to the legend, a phoenix turned into a beautiful young girl, came to the village, and married a young man. They loved each other and lived in bliss for a hundred years. After the young man grew old and died, she turned back into a phoenix and, with loud wails of grief, flew back up into the mountains.

"Does the phoenix live on our side of the mountains?" Long always asked.

"Yes, but we don't know where," Grandma replied every time. She also said that once there was an enormous fire in the village. Just as the villagers were about to abandon their homes and flee, a large bird of seven colors flew through the dark smoke, and wherever its wings flapped, the flames were extinguished. In gratitude to the phoenix—and in the hope that she would live there forever—they renamed the village Phoenix Home.

"Have you ever seen a phoenix, Grandma?"

"How could I? It was such a very long time ago. Besides, it is just a story."

Long loved this story.

She spent all day admiring the feather, and an idea grew in her mind, like grass peeking out after a spring rain, shy and irrepressible.

II. Seeking the Phoenix

Long set out early one morning, while her grandmother was still dreaming and her parents were away visiting relatives. There was no one to stop her.

She left a note that said, "Grandma, I am off to search for the phoenix. Don't worry—I'll come home." Carrying a sack of boiled potatoes and sweet potatoes on her back, she headed into the mountains, following the stream uphill.

The stream brought the feather down to the village, she thought, *so if I trace its path, I will find the phoenix.*

The stream danced merrily along, sometimes revealing its width in a mirage of iridescence, sometimes hiding in the rocks and tall grasses.

The nine-year-old clutched the feather tightly in one hand as she picked her way through thorny undergrowth, crossed rills and crevices, and clambered over enormous rocks. Her small braids came loose and her trousers tore in several places.

Near a low bush she came upon two snakes, one black and one blue green. She stopped and did not move at all, even when they crawled slowly past her feet and finally slithered away.

Tired, she settled herself on a mossy rock to rest and nibbled on a sweet potato. She picked several brightly colored wildflowers and arranged them in a bunch with the phoenix feather. She did not feel lonely or frightened—she thought only of the phoenix and the joy she would feel when she saw her.

She walked onward and didn't stop until darkness had descended upon the woods, and her eyes could no longer find the stream. Long looked around, realized she couldn't see anything, and cried out. She wailed louder and louder, even louder than the sound of the rushing water.

After a time, she grew weary from crying, opened her eyes, and dried them with the feather. How soft and smooth it was! A phoenix feather.

Suddenly, the river brightened—as bright as if the moon had fallen into the water, or as if a thousand stars had tumbled in, or as if all the droplets of water had turned into fireflies. A shoal of fish swam toward the surface, leaping over stones, stirring up silver splashes as though saying to her, "Hurry, hurry. Don't stop!"

"Oh!" Long's mouth opened in delight, for the bright water was showing her the way. She slipped through grass and trees, hopped over rills and crevices, clambered over huge rocks, and walked the entire night away. At dawn, the stream returned to normal, and Long made her way onward.

Led by the stream, she walked and walked for several days and nights.

At a deep pool she stopped. The water was crystal clear, and from its depths rose a trail of bubbles like huge transparent eyes. All around the pool was a clearing, filled with stones. At the center of the open area, a large pile of dried branches gave off a pleasant scent.

But where was the phoenix? Long had finally reached the source of the stream, and she had no idea where to go next. Looking at the feather in her hand, she sat at the edge of the pool, gulped down some water, and somehow drifted off to sleep.

III. The Eye of the Stream (The Spring)

In her dreams, the bubbling source of the stream spoke to her:

Child, I am a very old spring—old enough to have forgotten how old I am. I am as old and as young as the phoenix you seek. We existed when these mountains rose up between the sky and the earth, before anyone lived in these mountains.

Back then, my friend the phoenix perched in tall trees, drank from mountain springs, ate wild fruits, sang in a clear voice, and soared across the sky, above mountaintops and the changing colors of the earth as seasons came and went. At some point, people came and built their houses of wood and stone. In the mountain valley, houses sprang up one by one, people grew up one by one, and soon your village was born.

My friend is a spirit of the sky and earth. She knew everything under the sky, yet she was a stranger to people and did not understand what kind of creatures they were. She nested in a high tree and studied the village and its people day after day, watching them being born, watching them grow and work, then watching them age and die. Ah, how lovely and how pitiful they were, how foolish and how wise!

My friend was aloof and had a proud heart. She kept herself apart from them, and yet was drawn to them. The more she watched them, the more curious she became. One day, she changed herself into a beautiful young woman and walked to the village.

The day she walked into the village, it was shrouded in white mist, and people only a few feet apart could hardly see each other. When a strange girl suddenly arrived, the villagers were very hospitable, especially the older ladies. They asked her where she was from and where she was going, but she shook her head and said nothing.

When it grew dark, a housewife took her home, cooked her dinner, and let her sleep under her roof, intending to have her son take their guest home the next morning. The young man was nineteen years old, handsome, and so shy that he didn't even dare to look at the girl. He asked her softly where she wanted to go, but she just shook her head and kept shaking it for days on end.

So the housewife let her stay at the house.

By day the young man went up the mountains to cut firewood, and in the evening when he returned, he tipped a handful of wild hawthorn berries into her palm.

She laughed as she ate them, and the sound of her laughter was bright and sweet. When the boy stopped in shock and stared at her, she laughed harder still.

"You ... can *laugh*?"

"And talk, too."

"So you're not ..."

"Mute? No. I ... my name is Phoenix. And you?"

"My name is Xiaoan."

Phoenix could speak but still refused to tell anyone where she came from or where she was going.

Xiaoan's mother, a kind and loving woman, said, "Stay as long as you like, until the day you want to leave."

Phoenix lived with them for half a year. She often thought of returning to the mountains, but every time she planned to take flight after dark, her wings would fold themselves away before her feet even left the ground. She wasn't sure why. In the mountain forest she had felt free, yet listless and lonely. In the village she found an indescribable warmth that attracted her and made her long to stay.

Every evening, Xiaoan poured the hawthorn berries he had picked into her cupped hands. As their fingers touched and their eyes met, a shimmering breeze flowed through her heart—and in that breeze, the birds sang.

"Will you marry my son?" Xiaoan's mother asked her one day.

Phoenix nodded.

After that, Phoenix never again thought of leaving, nor did she tell Xiaoan of her true self: that she was a phoenix, more used to flying than walking, more used to perching on high branches than being on solid ground. That was why she seemed so clumsy and ignorant and did not know how to do anything. Sometimes she knocked over things around the house.

Xiaoan always smiled and never scolded her.

Slowly Phoenix learned to wash and cook and spin, while Xiaoan farmed and hunted and cut firewood. They were together day and night.

The flaming red azaleas blossomed and died. The reed flowers turned white and fluttered away. In the mountain village surrounded by white mist, Xiaoan grew old, and Phoenix aged herself along with him.

They lived together for one hundred years. One hundred years in the world is a good, long time. Even so, all such things must come to an end—and Phoenix, no matter how magical she was, could do nothing to change it.

IV. The Phoenix

One morning, Xiaoan did not wake up.

At his grave, Phoenix cried until she lost her voice, and then she wept blood. Her life was eternal, and Xiaoan would never return. With a bird's cry of mourning, she unfurled her wings, leapt into the sky, and circled in midair above the village. Only then did the people learn that she was a phoenix. On that day, the mountains and plains were crystal clear. A wall of cold air froze the mist onto the grass and trees, glazing each one to look like a carving of ice or jade, like a sculpture in a dream, and the phoenix disappeared into the rolling mountains.

The bird's longing for Xiaoan led her to stand guard over the village. Phoenix watched over it and kept it safe and peaceful, yet she could never shake off her grief. Her feathers fell out one by one, and no new ones grew in. Eventually, she had only one feather left and could not fly. No one who saw her would have recognized her as a phoenix. She dwelled in sorrow day and night, spring and autumn, one by one.

One day she awoke and wondered how she could possibly guard Xiaoan's village in her present condition.

"O Eye of the Spring," she said to me, "you have seen everything—my greatest joys and my deepest sorrows. It is time for me to bathe in fire and be reborn."

I was glad for her.

She gathered fragrant tree branches day by day and piled them into a high mound to make the blaze that would give her new life. But her beak was no longer hard enough to strike a spark against the rocks. Without a spark, there would be no flame. Without a flame there would be no fire to set the branches ablaze. Without a fire there would be no rebirth! All she could do was wait for a thunderbolt from the sky to strike the dry branches. She waited year after year.

Some time ago I asked her if there was any other solution. Ah, if only there was! I could think of nothing.

Plucking the last feather from her body, she tossed it into the stream and said, "Someone will pick it up. Someone will come to find me and help me light the branches. I believe it!"

I sighed. Alas, what a faint hope it is!

I didn't expect you. But you came—a little girl like you! Well, since you are here, strike a spark with a stone. Just one spark is enough to light the pile of branches. Please, light it quickly ...

V. The Flames

Disoriented, Long awoke with tears at the corners of her eyes and said to herself, *What a strange dream I had.* Her gaze fell on the large pile of branches beside the pool. It was silent, as if waiting for something. She gazed down into the pool. From the bottom, a constant stream of bubbles rose to the surface with a gurgle, like the voice that had spoken in her dream.

Surrounding the deep pool was a circle of empty, rocky ground. In the distance lay the forest, and there was not a breath of wind. Long tugged a large handful of dried grass from the ground and went to the pile of branches. She chose two rocks, set one on the grass, held the other in her hand and swung it down hard. Her hands were not strong and she didn't make a single spark for quite some time. But she did not give up. She raised her arm high, gathered all her strength, and brought the rock down harder, again and again and a—oh, a spark! The tiny spark bounced and ignited a fire in the dried grass. A small flame from the dried grass jumped to a branch. The small flame jumped again and again. Many small flames gathered into a large flame, crackling, crack-ling, *crackle, crackle, crackle, crackle, crackle, crackle, crackle, crackle, crackle, crackle-crackle-crackle-crackle-crackle-crackle-crackle-crackle-crackle—*
The whole pile burst into flame, and the flames rose

high into the air.

"Close your eyes, I'm here. Close your eyes now, I don't want to be seen. Please go far away and turn your back ..."

Ah, is it the voice of the phoenix? It must be! Long obediently walked away, turned her back, and shut her eyes. In fact, she very much wanted to look, but she did not let herself peek, knowing that a bald phoenix would not wish to be seen.

Ch-ch-ch, went the bird's footsteps. *Swish, whoosh, thump*, went the sound of the phoenix jumping onto a tree branch.

"What a good girl you are. You can turn around now and open your eyes."

Long looked back and saw the flames ripple in a graceful dance, and in the golden flames a slender, beautiful figure also danced with swaying, elegant movements.

Perhaps I'll turn to ash,
Perhaps I'll be reborn.
The fire burns everything,
Burns my body and soul,
All the joy and sorrow,
I don't forget,
I won't forget.
I want to be born anew.
I want to be reborn.

Is that Phoenix singing? Does the fire hurt? She must be in such pain! Teardrops rolled down Long's cheeks, and through the veil of her tears, she saw the figure of the phoenix fade, becoming more and more transparent, and finally merging with the flames.

The branches burned for quite some time before they went out, leaving behind a pile of hot ashes and plumes of white smoke.

"Where are you, Phoenix?" Long shouted, almost in tears.

VI. Phoenix Home

A high, clear cry resounded from the earth and sky, and instantly the ashes danced like snowflakes. A large dazzling bird rose from the ground into the air. She circled once, twice, three times, trailing her lush tail feathers across Long's face and eyes.

"Ah, Phoenix, I see you, I see you!" Long shouted happily.

The phoenix flew over her head, and Long tipped her head back to see better. She lay down on the ground with her face to the sky and looked and looked and laughed and cried ...

"Long, wake up! How did you get here? Wake up. What are you doing here all by yourself? Five days and nights —and such a small child!"

Long opened her eyes and saw her father, along with a group of uncles from the village.

Many, many years later, when Long became an adult, she was too old to remember whether her search for the phoenix had been real or a dream. So she told it to her children as if it was a story and was surprised when they clamored to go searching for the phoenix with her.

"You believe it?"

"We do!"

Long smiled, gathered the children into her arms, and hugged them. "I believe it too."

And why not believe? Believe that there is a phoenix who has lived in these mountains since long, long ago, and will live here for a very long time to come. How beautiful, even if—even if it is only a story!

ARE YOU A STAR?

I

A row of black cats sat on the windowsill.

Each was the size of a fist, and their silent, golden eyes stared at Xiaji. When he opened his eyes from a bottomless sleep, he met their deep gazes, and a tingle ran from his scalp down his spine.

Last night, had he been in his own house, or deep in the wilderness? It had seemed like a dream, but an extra cat sitting on the windowsill proved that last night's events had really happened.

For seven nights in a row now, just as Xiaji was drifting off to sleep, he heard a long, drawn-out sound like a cat purring. Xiaji had heard cats purr before—the sound reminded him of an endless train rumbling deep inside the little animal.

As if in a trance, he saw a dark green train rushing through the remote wilderness, spangled with dew and starlight and the fragrance of grasses, coming out of the wilderness toward his city and heading straight toward him. It sped past fields, through his city, right through the walls of his house as if they didn't exist, and stopped directly in front of him. The door of the train car banged open.

Xiaji jumped aboard. The passenger car was empty inside, except for him and one seat. The door clanged shut and the train chugged forward. Xiaji didn't panic. He leaned against a window and stared out at the darkness. The night and the lights and the houses blurred together into one. Soon there was only darkness and nothing left to see.

Perhaps a minute had passed, or perhaps an hour—there was no way of knowing—before a yellow half-moon appeared on the dark glass. The train once again traveled through the vast wilderness. Clusters of trees cast ghostly blue shadows, a winding river shone like a silver ribbon, and the sounds of sleepless bugs and birds floated in through the window.

The train suddenly slowed down and came to a stop. The door opened by itself, and Xiaji jumped off.

When he got off the train, he was stunned by the myriad stars in the sky. Never had he seen such a spectacular starry display—in his city or in his memory. Against the black sky, each star was clear, like a grain of salt or a diamond, bright and dense. For the first time Xiaji saw the Milky Way and the Big Dipper.

Beneath the starry sky were trees and grass, soil and stones, hills and streams, stars and moonlight, vastness and silence, mystery and the unknown.

II

The long, dark train lay in the depths of nowhere, wrapped up in a thin mist, as if it felt tired. Xiaji walked several steps around it, his heart pounding with excitement and wonder. He didn't dare go too far from the train and looked back every few steps to see if the door was open.

He heard a thin cry near his heels, and he turned to see a small black kitten with surprisingly large golden eyes on its tiny face. Xiaji bent down, took it in his hands, and noticed a star-like glimmer in its eyes. The little thing looked back at Xiaji and meowed pitifully, as if to say, "Take me away, take me away."

The train suddenly let out a *whooooo*, and the door shook as if it was about to close, so Xiaji scooped up the kitten and jumped aboard. The train started, left the wilderness, drove into the city, and finally stopped at Xiaji's window. He stepped off.

In the morning he awoke and was just about to comment on what a strange dream he had last night, when he saw a small black cat on his windowsill. What was going on? Oh—the window was half open, so maybe the little fellow had slipped in during the night! Was it just a coincidence with his dream?

"Hi. Where did you come from?" Xiaji held out his hand, but the cat jumped down from the windowsill and darted under the bed. No matter what he did, it still refused to come out. He tried tempting it with food and water to no avail.

What Xiaji didn't expect was that something similar would happen every night that followed.

Now another black cat sat on his windowsill.

The cats were careful to stay away from him. Whenever he tried to approach or touch them, they nimbly avoided his fingers.

But things were far from over. The rumbling purr would come each night and so would the train, and whether Xiaji wanted to or not, he jumped on and brought back a cat from the wilderness.

He tried staying awake the entire night, but no matter how hard he tried, his thoughts became blurry from the strange rumbling purr, and off he would ride on the train into the wilderness. As days passed, the number of cats in his room steadily grew: his windowsill, floor, desk, shelves and dresser were all crowded with black cats. They sat in row upon row, their eyes staring at him like a sea of golden stars. But the moment anyone came into his room, they disappeared in a flash, and he had no idea where they hid. More than once Xiaji told his parents about the wilderness, the train, and the cats. The three of them had searched the house together, but his parents never saw even the shadow of a black cat.

At night, Xiaji climbed onto the roof. The cats followed him and sat nearby. He felt a bit scared of them. At the same time, he was filled with curiosity and a puzzling sense of closeness to them. Together, they stared up at the pitifully few stars in the sky. As they stargazed, a dark green train arrived, bathed in dew and starlight and the fragrance of grasses. It halted in midair, opened its doors, and let him enter.

There were far too many cats to squeeze into Xiaji's house....

III

That night there was purring, but no train arrived from the wilderness. Xiaji slept deeply and dreamed that the cats jumped on his bed and squirmed under his body one by one. Like ants moving a piece of candy, they carried him out the window and into the vast night.

When he opened his eyes, he found himself in the wilderness lying on dirt and rocks. A few long-winged insects hopped around him, flower petals fell on him, his clothes were damp with dew, and he held a slender stalk of green grass in his mouth. From far away came the sound of wind over water. The sky was of full of bright, cheerful stars. The night was empty, quiet, and so very lonely.

He pinched himself hard on the arm. It hurt, so he wasn't dreaming.

He got up and climbed a small hill, from which he could see better. The wilderness seemed larger and more savage than he had seen it before. He saw brambles and dark, dense forests, and murky bubbling swamps. The place frightened him and he did not want to stay long. Just then, he saw the train in the mist a short way off, looking long and solid and dependable. He ran toward it, though its doors were shut as if it was taking a nap. He patted all the doors and windows, but it made no noise.

He could only walk aimlessly, not knowing how to get out of the wilderness and back home.

At dawn the sun was so bright that it stung his eyes

and he was forced to screw them shut and rest against a tree. He fell asleep, and when he woke it was night again. A few ants crawled around on him. He was hungry, so he followed the sound of flowing water and found a river where he drank his fill. A tree on the river-bank was heavy with fruit, some of which had fallen to the ground. He picked up a few pieces, washed them, and filled his stomach with them.

At daybreak it was blindingly bright again, and he fell asleep in a thicket.

In this way, sleeping by day and roaming the wilderness by night, he passed more days than he cared to count.

Loneliness was driving him mad. He shouted at the train and pounded on it with a rock, desperately trying to wake it up, but to no avail. He didn't understand what was going on.

His supply of fruit under the tree was almost depleted, and soon he would have to climb it if he wanted to eat. Xiaji did not know how to climb trees. He realized with horror that the wilderness was about to swallow him up, and yet the stars in the sky had never twinkled so merrily.

IV

Under the starlight Xiaji suddenly saw something huge—an enormous cat, taller than any tree on the plains, its body darker than night, its tail thicker than a python. He saw it from a distance. At first he was afraid and wanted to run away, but fear vanished in an instant and was replaced by a deep sense of longing. He wanted to move closer to it. Nothing could be more terrible than the loneliness of this wasteland.

He sidled closer to it, step by step, until he was right beneath its large body. He raised his face to it with a tentative "Hi." As the cat turned and lowered its head, Xiaji saw a pair of huge, sad eyes.

"Hi," he said again.

But the cat had looked away and settled back into its original position. It sat with its front legs together and upright, its hind legs curled under against the ground, while the tail wrapped halfway around its body like some sort of snake.

Xiaji reached out and touched its tail.

The enormous cat straightened its hind legs, arched its back, and left.

"Hey!" Xiaji looked awhile at the colossal shadow it cast on the ground and followed it with determination. He felt his loneliness ease somewhat, but the cat had no intention of letting him follow for long. It sprang quickly and nimbly, sprang over the river, sprang over the swamp, and in the blink of an eye was out of sight in the mountains.

Xiaji sighed in frustration.

His next few days in the wilderness were different, however. He often saw the figure of the enormous cat, still some distance away but never far from his sight. Although it was large and black, he didn't fear it. Its eyes gathered twinkling starlight. Bit by bit, Xiaji approached it, and bit by bit it moved away. It remained at a distance, yet never out of sight.

Xiaji hoped to gain its trust, hoped to be closer to it, so they could rely on each other and he would have the strength to face this wilderness without being alone and helpless.

The fruit that had fallen on the riverbank had all been eaten.

There was plenty on the tree, but Xiaji could not reach it. He held the trunk of the tree and shook it hard, but he couldn't move it an inch. He threw rocks up into the branches, but none of the fruit fell.

He was very hungry, and afraid that he might starve to death.

When he felt completely helpless, the black cat strolled over and smacked the crown of the tree a few times with its front paws as if playing a drum. Fruit fell to the ground like rain.

Xiaji was surprised and grateful. "Oh, thank you!"

The cat moved away as if it had not heard.

This gave Xiaji new hope. He believed that the cat was his guardian in the wilderness. Although the "guardian" felt cold and distant, Xiaji found fresh courage to survive.

Whenever he went too long without seeing the cat, Xiaji felt empty inside, fear and loneliness raking his heart with sharp claws.

But the big cat never let him get too close.

V

The swamp gurgled and bubbled. The bubbles crackled and burst into white foam, as if there were a carnival, as if demons waited in the depths of the swamp to welcome Xiaji warmly into the black mud and into their arms.

Yes, he was trapped.

One day, rendered blind and dizzy by harsh sunlight, he stumbled into the swamp.

At first the squelchy mud and water only reached his calves, then he sank past his knees and up to his waist. He could not pull himself free. Day turned into night, and night turned into day.

The giant cat squatted on a rock close by and watched him.

"Help me," Xiaji said to it.

The cat either couldn't hear him or couldn't understand his words. It sat without moving, looking at Xiaji with huge, sad eyes. It watched and did nothing.

But Xiaji had hope. He believed it would save him, and it was certainly capable of saving him. He had seen it leap over the swamp with his own eyes. Ever since the cat helped him get fruit from the tree, he had considered it his guardian in the wasteland.

He had been stuck in the swamp for four days and four nights. He did not sink any further, but neither could he climb out.

"You will save me, won't you?"

The giant cat looked silently back at him. Xiaji was getting weak, but the cat never moved.

The stars came out every night. Starlight touched the eyes of the giant cat and Xiaji.

On the sixth day, Xiaji was still in the swamp and the giant cat still looked at him in the same way. Xiaji suddenly realized that the cat would not save him. It was silently waiting for him to die.

The thought plunged Xiaji into an abyss of terror and despair.

He wept bitterly and begged, "Help me. I don't want to die—please save me."

The cat was unmoved. Its eyes were sorrowful, but it clearly did not wish to do anything for him.

It must have the hardest, coldest heart in the world,

Xiaji thought. Finally, he was desperate, knowing he would die there.

On the seventh night, he looked up at the stars. How warm and bright they were. Xiaji's breath was ragged, his mind at the edge of delirium. That was when he remembered a kitten named Star from seven years ago when he was six. He had not thought of it for a long time.

VI

That winter morning, Xiaji was home alone. Papa and Mama were out. He went downstairs to fetch some milk and saw a tiny cat watching him from outside.

It was only the size of his fist, thin and ugly with dirty white fur. Its large eyes opened wide and it meowed weakly at him.

Xiaji opened the door, and the kitten jumped into the house.

"You must be hungry. Where are you from?"

He poured it a bowl of milk, and it licked the dish clean. He tore off a hunk of bread for it and watched as it gulped it down. Then it curled up by his feet and fell asleep.

Xiaji sat on the ground, hardly daring to breathe for fear of awakening the little creature. It was such a small, pitiful thing to be lost out in the big world.

The cat slept very well, and its rumbling purr sounded like a distant train. Xiaji fell asleep listening to it.

They woke at the same time. The kitten had eaten so well and slept so well that it became much livelier and began to play with him.

"Your eyes are as bright as stars," Xiaji said. "So am I going raise you? Should I call you Star?"

They played together and had a happy day. When Papa and Mama came home, Xiaji told them, "I want to raise a Star."

"What star?"

"*It*, of course."

"Ugh, where did you find such a dirty, smelly cat? Throw it out," Mama cried.

"Let me keep Star, Mama. It is so small. It will get sick and starve or freeze to death if we chase it out."

"Star? Is that what you called it? You shouldn't just give something a name without thinking, child. You'll get attached if you do."

"I am *already* attached, Mama. Let me raise it."

"No. I don't like cats. There's no place for cats in our family."

Xiaji turned to his father.

"You can keep it," Papa said, "but it must stay in the basement."

The *basement*? No—Xiaji hated it there! It was dark

and crowded with strange debris, and there were bugs, long worms, and rats crawling around.

Papa also said that all expenses—cat food, litter, shots for Star—would have to be paid out of Xiaji's allowance.

"Oh! But that would empty my piggy bank," he said in distress.

Softly Mama said, "Xiaji is a good boy and always listens to his parents, doesn't he? If you obey me, I'll buy you that remote-controlled airplane you wanted."

Ah—Xiaji had been wanting that airplane for such a long time! "Okay," he said. "I'll obey."

In order to keep the kitten from finding its way back, Papa drove the car all the way out to the edge of town to an empty lot overgrown with weeds. It was a wilderness out there, piled high with garbage. Xiaji placed Star gently on the ground and quickly dove back into the car. The cat meowed at him. The car drove, and the kitten tried to follow, running and stumbling as it went.

In the darkness, Xiaji soon lost sight of it, and he wept.

"Will Star die?"

"No. It will become a strong wildcat."

"Of course."

Mama's words made Xiaji feel much better. He wouldn't have to walk down the stairs into the dark, dirty basement for Star, or spend all his money. He had the best remote-controlled airplane. Mama had said that Star would be fine, and he chose to believe it. Before long, Xiaji forgot Star.

VII

Xiaji spoke to himself as much as to the enormous cat as he told the story of Star.

"I abandoned it in the wilderness, and it must have been so afraid—like I am right now. I shouldn't have given it up like that. I never forgot."

The cat seemed to be listening, but even if it was, it might not have understood.

But Xiaji could see crystal-clear liquid streaming from its eyes, and as starlight touched the tears, they turned into stars.

His heart quaked. He had seen something familiar in those eyes.

"Are you Star?" he asked out loud. But it couldn't be Star. His Star was white all over.

The enormous cat suddenly leapt into the air and as it passed over Xiaji's head, it reached out with its front paws, grabbed his shoulders and pulled him from the mud. Placing Xiaji beside the river, it jumped to the opposite bank, and disappeared into the depths of the wilderness.

"Wait! *Are* you Star?" Xiaji asked over and over.

But the cat did not reappear.

He drank water, ate some fruit, and bathed in the river. From behind him came the rumble of a train starting up, and he ran to it. The passenger car door opened—it was awake. As soon as Xiaji leapt in, the door closed and the train began to move.

Like a star falling from the sky in the early morning, Xiaji landed on his windowsill with a *tap*. Hearing the noise, Papa and Mama raced in to ask why in the world he had climbed onto the windowsill at this time of day. There was neither worry nor joy on their faces at their reunion.

Xiaji told them of his adventure in the wilderness. They said that they had heard quite a few cats yowling outside last night.

Last night? Had his adventures lasted only one night?

Epilogue

From then on, Xiaji never again heard that strange rumbling purr in the night. No dark trains ever came to carry him away to a wilderness. There was not a single black cat left anywhere in the house either.

His adventures ended as incredibly as they had begun.

He thought often of that enormous black cat, with

its sad, helpless eyes. Why did it catch him and take him to the wilderness, and why did it let him out?

It looked nothing like the kitten called Star, yet Xiaji always thought of them at the same time.

Is Star doing well? Did it really grow up to become a strong wildcat?

CHIM NEY

Chim was seven when she met a ghost with insomnia.

She met it right in her adobe house.

It was almost dark, and after dinner her parents had gone to join the fun under the big locust tree in the village. Chim squatted in front of the old clay stove, trying to pull out a freshly cooked sweet potato. All of a sudden, *poof*, a flurry of ashes blew into her face, making her cough and sputter, and bringing tears to her eyes.

The ashes had hardly settled when someone crawled out of the stove—*uuuhhhhh!*—wearing a blue satin hat, a blue satin shirt, blue satin trousers, and blue satin shoes. Strangely enough, there was not a speck of dust on his fine blue clothes.

"Who ... who are you?" Chim asked.

"I ... I am a ghost," Blue Satin replied.

"Ghost? What is a ghost?" Chim continued.

"Ghost? A ghost is something everyone is afraid of," Blue Satin said.

Chim became even more curious. "Do you eat people?"

"I don't eat people, but whenever people mention me, their legs shake and their faces go white. Isn't that scary?" the ghost asked with a smile.

Chim gave a little sigh. "I don't know if you're scary, but why did you climb through my chimney?"

Now it was the ghost's turn to sigh. He said, "Oh dear, oh dear, I have insomnia—very, very serious insomnia. Do you know what insomnia is, little girl?"

"No."

"Insomnia is when you can't sleep."

"Oh. But why can't you sleep?"

"Because I am too clever, so clever that other ghosts can't understand me. And I am too lonely, so lonely that no other ghosts want to keep me company. So I got depressed, and then I couldn't sleep. Do you know what it's like to have insomnia?"

"No," Chim answered honestly.

"It is exhausting to talk to a little girl. This must be what it feels like to go crazy—it's crushing! It's dreadful, just dreadful!"

"Oh. Maybe it really is."

"Right. By the way, I'm calling myself 'Sleep' for now because I want to sleep so badly. I met an excellent ghost doctor earlier today, and he told me that the best way to cure sleeplessness is to find a warm, smoking chimney at dusk and hang upside down in it until four the next morning." The ghost in blue satin pointed to her chimney. "If I hang in there for eighty-eight years, my insomnia is bound to be cured!"

"Oh. I see. Then why did you drop down here just now and scare me?"

"I'm sorry—it's my first time hanging upside down. I'm not very good at it yet."

"A ghost dangling upside down in my chimney? What fun! Do you like my house's chimney?"

"Very much. It's warm and cozy."

"Great! Then come here every day, and don't go into anyone else's chimney."

"Would you let me borrow your chimney to hang in *for eighty-eight years*?"

"Of course," Chim said with absolute confidence.

"You are such a good girl—I want to grant you a wish, no matter how big it is!" Sleep looked very solemn.

"Really?"

"Really. Speak up—ghosts don't like to owe anyone favors, much less a little girl."

"I want long, long eyelashes that flutter like the wings of a butterfly."

"That's it? Well, it's too small a wish. In fact, you could ask for a lot of gold or a nice house. I'm worried you'll regret this one day."

The blue-satin ghost called Sleep lifted his wide sleeves and with a gentle flick, Chim got a pair of long eyelashes that raised a tiny breeze whenever they fluttered.

She touched her eyes and giggled with joy. "I must look very pretty."

"Yes, beautiful." Sleep laughed with her.

"I'll pinky swear never to forget …"

"Don't forget to cook dinner every day and keep the chimney warm."

"Okay."

"Every day for eighty-eight years."

"Okay."

"…"

Though they hooked their pinkies together and swore a solemn oath, the ghost called Sleep was rather worried. The more easily she gave her word, the more uneasy he felt.

Of course the chimney stayed warm every day.

After all, her Mama cooked three tasty meals a day

—breakfast, lunch, and dinner—and never missed a meal.

When Papa and Mama went out for a stroll each night after dinner, Chim would say to the chimney, "Sleep, are you there?"

"Yes, but please don't disturb me—I am trying to sleep."

So Chim would stay quiet. Just thinking about the ghost hanging upside down in her chimney was excitement enough.

The funny thing was that Sleep often lost his grip and fell down the chimney, right into the ashy stove. He would climb out with an embarrassed air and chat amiably with Chim for a while.

"Hanging upside down in a chimney must be exhausting."

"On the contrary, it is quite cozy—especially the warm feeling that makes you forget your sorrows."

"Is it really dark in there?"

"It's dark, but when you look up you can always see a star."

"Can I try it?"

"Of course you can't."

"..."

When Chim was sixteen, her loving parents passed away, one after the other.

She lived alone in the little adobe cottage, enduring grief every day. One day she even thought of following her parents to another world, but Sleep stopped her.

"Don't go, little girl," he said. "Did you forget our eighty-eight-year agreement? How could you bear to leave me with a cold chimney?"

Chim often forgot to eat breakfast or lunch, but she never forgot to cook dinner.

At dusk she sat beside the clay stove.

"I am here, Chim." Sleep's muffled voice drifted down the chimney, buzzing slightly.

"Oh. Is it warm in there?"

"It's warm."

"Oh. Then I won't bother you." Chim stopped talking, and so did Sleep.

But Sleep began to hum in a thick, rough voice. The song he hummed was not at all in tune, and the only song he sang was, "Twinkle, twinkle, glitter bright, fill the sky with sparkling light, shine little stars ..."

He hummed quite earnestly and kept humming until gradually Chim fell asleep.

At the "shine little stars" part of Sleep's tune, Chim fell into a sweet slumber, like a child who still had her parents' love.

Slowly Chim emerged from grief.

Chim was soon old enough to marry.

Many came to propose to her, for she was a beautiful young woman, but eventually they all chose to leave.

Every day, some people arrived and some left.

At last, tired of explaining, Chim posted a notice on her front door. Many people took one look at the sign and left, shaking their heads.

One day, a slim young man was passing by and read the sign on the door. He smiled slightly.

The notice said, "If you can't guarantee that you'll live in this adobe cottage for the rest of your life, then go away."

The young man knocked on the door and went in.

In front of him was a fair young girl, with long eyelashes that fluttered like the wings of a butterfly, like tiny fans creating a light breeze. For an instant, the boy almost forgot how to breathe.

Chim lowered her eyes. "You are ...?"

"I am Ney. As in 'chimney,'" the young man answered.

Chim couldn't help but chuckle. "Could there be such a strange name in all the world? I am Chim."

"Ah." The young man laughed too. "So together our names are Chimney."

Red clouds came to their cheeks as they both blushed.

Chim was twenty-two. So was Ney.

Together they lived in the old house. They married and had a happy life.

On the night of their wedding, Sleep stopped humming the out-of-tune "Twinkle, Twinkle." He could finally hang wholeheartedly in the chimney to cure his insomnia.

At first, Chim did not mention Sleep to her husband, worried that he might be frightened; until one day, Sleep tumbled down the chimney again. Humming, he climbed out of the stove and heard a cry of fright.

It was Ney.

In a panic, Sleep scrambled back into the chimney and hung upside down, thinking sadly that his pleasant days here would now end. If Chim asked him to leave and never come back, he would go, although he would have to find a new chimney and begin his eighty-eight-year cure all over again.

Ney fell ill.

When he recovered, Chim anxiously explained her eighty-eight-year promise.

"Did you really only ask for long eyelashes?" Ney asked.

"Yes."

"Oh, darling, that is so cute." Ney kissed her on the forehead. "I will keep this promise with you."

As the old house grew ever older, it was not just Chim, but Chim and Ney that greeted Sleep every day at dusk.

"Sleep, are you here yet?"

"Yes, yes—but please don't disturb me."

Chim and Ney would look at each other and smile.

Sweet days passed as quickly as flowing water.

When Chim was thirty-five years old, she fell asleep one night and did not wake up again. The sun is still blushing.

Only Ney and two children were left in the old house.

Ney lived with his grief every day. He sometimes forgot to make breakfast or lunch, but he never forgot to cook dinner.

He would sit beside the clay oven when he was done cooking.

Sleep's voice drifted down from the chimney. "I am here, Ney."

"Is it warm enough?"

"It's warm."

"Oh. That is good."

"Let me sing to you." Sleep's music flowed from the chimney, thick and rough and off-key. "Twinkle, twinkle, glitter bright, fill the sky with sparkling light, shine little stars ..." His voice had grown worse for more than a decade.

"Chim said you used to sing to her. Is that true?"

"Yes, right up to the day you married, and she wasn't alone anymore."

"Was it the same song?"

"Yes, it's the only one I know."

"Then sing it and think of Chim. My heart will feel better."

Sleep's song rolled down from the chimney over and over, and Chim was in the song. Ney slowly fell asleep, as if Chim was right beside him.

Ney's family came to him and said, "Chim is gone. Why are you staying here?"

Ney refused to leave.

Many young women came hoping to marry him, enchanted by his handsome face and his devotion.

Ney shook his head.

More than ten years passed. The two children grew up, built new houses, and moved away.

Ney lived alone. He always felt that Chim was sitting in a corner of the old cottage, watching him with a smile and fluttering her long lashes.

Even Sleep tried to persuade him. "Go live with your children. That eighty-eight-year promise was between Chim and me. You don't have to stay here."

Ney smiled. "I am protecting Chim's oath. Her promise is my promise."

By now he no longer needed Sleep's off-key version of "Twinkle, twinkle" to keep him company at night. He slowly left his grief behind.

✳ ⁀⁀ ∞ ⁀⁀ ✳

Ten years passed, then twenty and thirty and forty. The old adobe cottage grew more and more dilapidated, and Ney had to fix it every day.

But the chimney always remained warm.

Whenever Sleep fell from his perch, they talked, and of course their talks were about Chim.

"Do you still think about her?" Sleep asked tentatively.

"Every minute."

"It must give your heart pain to think of her so often when she is gone."

"No, no, not pain. Thoughts of her keep my heart warm." Ney's smile flowed from his wrinkles.

"Actually, I miss her often, and when I think of it, I want to cry." Sleep covered his eyes and scrambled back into the chimney.

Fifty years passed, then sixty.

Ney lived alone in the little adobe cottage for sixty years. One man's sixty years can feel longer than six hundred.

There were almost no such adobe cottages left in the village. They either crumbled away or were demolished. Beautiful new buildings went up one by one.

Of course, none of them had chimneys.

Why would they need them? New gas stoves replaced the old clay models, and fumes were whisked up plastic shafts right above them.

Only one chimney remained in the village.

Perhaps nobody recalled the wreaths of cook-smoke that had encircled the village at dusk many years ago.

Ney's chimney smoked at dawn, at noon, and at dusk. Soft pale wreaths of smoke rose as usual, quietly telling the story. It was always warm.

Ney fell and hurt his leg once when he was collecting firewood up on the mountains.

His children and grandchildren tried to force him to come live with them, but he struggled to return to the old cottage.

Every evening after dinner, he sat on a stool by the clay stove where he used to sit with Chim.

"Sleep, are you there?"

"Yes, yes, but please don't disturb me."

Ney smiled to himself.

One day as Ney sat by the stove, Sleep once again fell headfirst down the chimney into the clay stove and scrambled out. Blue satin hat, blue satin shirt, blue satin trousers, and blue satin shoes.

Sleep sighed. "You look so old."

"Ninety-five, if I remember correctly. You haven't changed the least bit."

"I'm a ghost. How could I be old?"

Ney said, "A person who is old is old."

Sleep lowered his head and rubbed both hands on the legs of his blue satin trousers, rubbing, rubbing.

"Sleep, if there's anything you want to say, just say it."

Sleep still hesitated. He didn't speak for a long time.

"I'll plug my ears if you don't talk."

Finally Sleep said, "My insomnia is cured."

"That's a good thing. Have you been hanging here for eighty-eight years?"

"Yes, exactly eighty-eight," Sleep said. "I don't know how to thank you and your chimney. I can grant you one wish, no matter how big."

"Oh. Thank you for keeping me company all these years. I have no wish except to see Chim."

Sleep said, "I probably won't be coming tomorrow. I probably won't be coming again. So I'll say goodbye."

Ney smiled and nodded. "Goodbye."

Sleep, in blue satin, whisked back into the stove, and "Goodbye" drifted down the chimney.

Ney sighed, long and deep. He lay on the bed, had a good stretch, and immediately fell asleep.

His body felt light and airy as it left the ground and floated up into the sky.

Before long, he saw a figure all in blue satin.

"Didn't you say goodbye?" Ney asked. "Why am I seeing you again?"

Sleep gave him a sly wink. "Yes. Maybe we'll see each other more often in the future."

Ney felt puzzled, but his body kept floating upward.

"Do you want to see Chim?" Sleep asked.

"Yes."

"Then I'll take you to her."

"Can you find her?"

"It's harder when you've been apart for sixty years—but we'll definitely find her."

Ney followed Sleep through the sky. They floated and floated.

Who knows how long they floated?

Suddenly, the figure in blue satin disappeared.

Ney was about to cry out when he saw before him a girl in fluttering skirts. How beautiful she was—especially her long lashes that fluttered like the wings of a butterfly, sending out a gentle breeze. Hadn't he been drawn to lashes like these decades ago?

"Is it Chim?"

"Is it Ney?"

"Chim, you still look twenty-two."

"So do you."

Ney touched his face in surprise and couldn't find a single wrinkle.

"I've been waiting for you."

"Me too."

"I've missed you."

"Me too."

They joined hands and looked into each other's faces for a long time.

"From now on, let's never be separated again."

"Never again."

With so much to say, they held hands and talked as they floated higher into the sky and into thicker clouds.

"Is Sleep cured of his insomnia?" Chim asked.

"He's cured," Ney answered.

"Thank you for keeping my eighty-eight-year promise."

"By protecting your oath, I was watching over you."

"I miss that old house so much."

"Me too."

The crimson face of the sun had just appeared over the old village where Chim and Ney had lived—

The last adobe cottage disappeared. *Whoosh.*

The last chimney also disappeared. *Whoosh.*

Disappeared quickly and cleanly, without a trace.

They had been there for so long, and then it seemed as if they had never existed.

PUBLISHER'S NOTE

The original text of this work was created in Chinese. The translator, editor, and publisher have made every effort to ensure that the English-language version is as accurate as possible and in keeping with the artistic intent of the author. Because this work reflects a different culture, some of the ideas and attitudes may be unfamiliar to the English-language audience.

ABOUT THE AUTHOR

Tang Tang, one of China's most celebrated authors of children's literature, began creating fairy tales in 2003. Her works often integrate traditional Chinese storytelling with Western fantasy elements, using vivid and humorous language to craft unique stories of wonder and magic.

She is a member of the Chinese Writers Association (and one of its first "National Reading Promoters"), vice chair of the Zhejiang Writers Association, and image spokesperson for reading in Zhejiang. Tang Tang has won numerous children's literature awards in China, including the Gold Award, and the National Outstanding Children's Literature Award—China's highest award in the field—for three consecutive years.

Among her best known works are "Hiding in Your Heart," "Kakasha the Water Sprite," "A Biography of the Incisor A Shang," and "Green Pearl." Her works have been translated into English, Japanese, Russian and many other languages.

www.ingramcontent.com/pod-product-compliance
Lightning Source LLC
Chambersburg PA
CBHW042033120726
47911CB00026B/720